HOOD SOUTHERN BELLE

D. WASHINGTON

HOOD SOUTHERN BELLE

D. WASHINGTON

Publisher:
MEWE, LLC
www.mewellc.com

First Edition

ISBN: 978-1-7334383-9-1

Library of Congress Control Number: 2020949011

For Worldwide Distribution
Printed in the USA

I would like to dedicate this book to my mom (R.I.P) for all of the lessons of hard work and perseverance. Thank you for teaching me to be bold and instilling in me that, "if you look good you feel good."

To my heartbeats and "Hunni Babies," had it not been for you, I would not have had the courage to write this book and explain my lessons. Thanks for pushing me to my full potential; I pray to give you back this same gift.

To my little sister...my brat, but always my friend. Thank you for being my soundboard for ideas and inspiration.

And to my Lord God and Savior who has seen me at my worst and at my best and loved me unconditionally when I didn't think I was lovable. Thank you for your grace and your mercy. I love you.
Your Word continues to inspire me...

I can do all things through Christ who strengthens me.
(Philippians 4:13)

God is good all the time and all the time god is good.
(Psalm 145.9)

Disclaimer Statement: I have tried to recreate events, locales and conversations from my memories of them. In order to maintain their anonymity in some instances, I have changed the names of individuals and places; I may have also changed some identifying characteristics and details such as physical properties, occupations and places of residence.

TABLE OF CONTENTS

Preface

Growing up I did not connect with my mother; I felt alienated because she presented herself as perfect. So, when I became a mother. I choose to be transparent in everything. I decided to write a journal for my daughter so when I go home to be with the Lord, she will know me, and thus, understand herself. When she got older, she found the journal and, after I explained what it was, she suggested that I write a book to not only help her but other girls who feel lost.

- D. Washington

1

My Family

Let me introduce myself. My official name is Denise Williams, but my nickname is Chocolate – Choc to friends. As you probably guessed, yassssss, I'm a proud dark-skinned sister. Don't hate it! Back in the day, it was all about "yella bone" sisters and brothers. Now dark skin is winning! I'm "paper-sack" brown, 5'4, 125 pounds, my natural hair in locks, with a nice onion booty, and a little gut that I'm not mad about because I love to eat! Plus, only a dog wants a bone. I would say my biggest asset is my big Kool-Aid smile and my genuine personality. However, my confidence was not always where it is now.

However, as the saying goes, when you have a lot of haters, they make you greater!

Everyone has a story and mine is about the "good girl" turned "bad girl," turned "good girl." I don't know why, especially us women tend to go chasing waterfalls, but always revert to who we are in our hearts.

I guess, what they say about generational curses is real…

###

My parents grew up in Port Arthur, Texas, right around the corner from one another, but they were complete opposites. My father's name was Lester Johnson, but they called him "Smooth." He was definitely a lady's man, 5'10, caramel skin toned with naturally curly hair. Although we did not get along at times, he is still to this very day, the coolest human being on earth to me. He never called anyone by their real name and used slang like, "What ya no good?," and "What up jack?" – the true definition of old school.

My mother, Diana Jackson, should have been a model, standing at 5'5 and 110 pounds. (How old was she, because 5'5' isn't tall) Her skin was almost bronze, and she had beautiful bone straight hair because of her Creole heritage. My mother and I were best friends; she shared everything with me. She had such a beautiful spirit!

I was conceived in the back seat of Lester's car, and it went something like this:

Lester: Aww, gurl, let me put the head in.

Diana: No, I'm scared; what if I get pregnant?

Lester: You can't get pregnant if I just put the head in.

Diana: Okay.

After about five pumps, Lester was done. He looked my mom square in the eyes and asked, "Hey, let my homeboy get some?"

This type of disrespect would be the norm for my mother for years to come. My share-cropping grandparents were devastated about the pregnancy. My parents were forced to have a "shotgun" wedding, where my grandpa literally held a shotgun to my father's head and forced my father to make his daughter an honest woman. This would be the start of a disrespectful, toxic relationship. Diana had seven initial months of pure hell with various women due to all of the infidelities of my father. My mother's parents could not do much to help her because they still had eight kids to raise. So, my father's sister Aileen sent for my mother to come live with her in Houston, Texas, until she had her baby to get away from all the stress and drama.

Three months premature, Denise Johnson arrived in Houston, Texas, at Jefferson Davis Hospital. Unfortunately, my lungs were not fully developed so I had to stay in the hospital for an additional three months. My aunt Aileen and my mother would take turns visiting me after they got off work, but my father was nowhere to be found. This would be the first of many occasions my dad would not be present.

Three years later, my sister Chrissy was born. She was a cute chubby little princess, but she hardly ever smiled. When it was just the two of us, she was bubbly and affectionate, and we would do everything together. I was very protective of her, and everyone knew it! Chrissy was a homebody, but on the rare occasions she came outside to play, she would always make a touchdown or homerun. It was an unwritten rule that when she got the ball, not a single person was allowed to touch her!

I also tried my best to protect her inside the house. When she would ask where our father was, or why our mom was so sad, I would make up an excuse so she wouldn't feel abandoned, like I did. That's what big sisters do – protect.

2

FRIENDS AND FOES

I grew up in the beautiful capital city of Austin, Texas, with so many hills that just about everyone used their parking brakes to stop the car from rolling when they parked. It never got too cold, but the summers could be unbearable, though as kids that never stopped us from having fun. If we weren't at Bartholomew's swimming pool, we were blocking traffic in our neighborhoods, playing football, kickball, dodge ball and any other ball you could think of from sun up to sun down.

A couple of weeks before school would start my parents would drive my sister and me to our grandparents' home to Port Arthur, Texas, – yes, "land of the trill, ya heard!" – to spend time with them. My favorite part of this four-hour drive was driving through Houston, Texas. Man, once we would enter Houston I would sit up, eyes wide, with my nose pressed to the window and admire the big bright lights, the big tall buildings and the cars going superfast on the big open highways. I guess the fact that I was actually born in Houston always gave me a feeling that one day I would be back for good.

Growing up in Austin wasn't half bad. I had great friends that made an impact on my life – some good, some bad. I met my first childhood bestie, Donna, when we moved to our new neighborhood in Colony Park. People often mistook us for sisters because we looked so much alike. We had instant chemistry. We liked the same foods and had similar tastes in clothes and music. Donna and I did stupid stuff like knocking on doors and saying, "My mama asked can we borrow an egg?" Then we'd take it to the railroad tracks across the way to see if it was really hot enough to fry an egg. We did dumb stuff like that all the time! She was the "Frick" to my "Frack." But our favorite pastime was when our parents let us spend the night at each other's house.

###

One day at Pearce Middle School, a new girl walked in the classroom. The teacher said, "Quiet down, class! I'd like everyone to give a big welcome to Lisa. Lisa comes from California and she will be joining us for the rest of the year." Now Lisa was a big girl; no, not big as in fat or heavy, but big as in 36C! She had on a real live adult bra! The first thing I thought was how could I get my poor training bra buds to look like that? Lisa was fifteen years old and in the 7th grade. I guess the schools must be hard in California because everything about Lisa seemed to be way mature. She just had a way about her; everything she did or said always had everyone on the edge of their seat. Even the boys appeared to be mesmerized!

Eventually, Donna, Lisa and I became the "It" click. We walked down the halls together, ate in the lunchroom together, and wore the same color shirts every day. We were the shezznix! Lisa was the first person to talk about sex, too. I don't know about

Donna, but I liked having Lisa around because she gave us a next level type of status. Lisa made us popular!

My mom, my sister and I were very close. My father would leave every year. I guess whatever was in those streets kept him busy six months out the year. I often wondered if he had a whole other family somewhere. Every time he left, my mom would vent to me because she was so sad. We were more like friends because my father ran away all of her friends. She would vent to me about my father's infidelities in detail. I even went to the clinic with her a couple of times to cure the latest STD he gave her. Being the protective big sister, my sister never knew why we were always at the clinic. We tried to keep her out of those conversations. Most of the time my little sister would stay in her room watching T.V. when she saw that my mom was having a "sad day." I loved my mother, and I would try to comfort her as best as I could although I was just a kid.

One day I convinced my mom into letting me have a sleepover. Of course, I invited Donna and Lisa. My mom ordered pepperoni pizza and sprite from Pizza Hut and we watched the popular show, *Last Dragon*, and scary movie, *Carrie,* until we fell asleep. I had a queen-sized bed, and in order for us to be comfortable, we had to sleep in a spooning position, Lisa on the left, Donna in the middle and me on the right. During the middle of the night, I felt Donna jump; then she jumped again. As, I turned my head to see what was going on, Donna whispered, "She's trying to goose me!"

"Goose you?" I said.

Donna said, "Yea, feeling on me. Let's trade spots."

I had no idea what Donna was talking about. I mean, we were in a small queen size bed, so of course, we are going to be touching one another. Donna knew I hated sleeping in the middle, but I was tired and didn't want to make it a big deal, so I switched places with her. I'm sure this made Lisa mad, because she made a frustrated noise, then got up and went to the restroom. That's when we noticed the sheer negligee Lisa had on. Once the restroom door was closed, Donna turned to me and whispered, "That girl tried to goose me!"

"SHUT UP!" I said.

"Yea she sure did, she…", Donna said.

Just then Lisa opened the door and came back in the room. Donna and I played sleep. After a while we all fell asleep, until I felt Lisa's hand on my breast. My eyes shot open! My body jumped just like Donna's did before. Lisa began to squeeze my nipples; I felt a tingling sensation down in my private parts, almost like I had to pee. I tried to play sleep and lightly pushed her hand away.

"What is she doing?" I thought.

I didn't want to get into it with Lisa because after all, she was my friend. So, I tried to ignore it and play it off. I moved closer to Donna. Lisa's hand traveled down to my private part.

As soon as I felt her finger traveling south, I jumped up and shouted, "WHAT ARE YOU DOING?"

I climbed over Donna and turned on the lights. Donna and I both jumped out of bed, staring wide eyed, waiting on a response from Lisa.

If looks could kill, Donna and I would have been dead on the spot!

Lisa, stood up and said, "If I knew y'all would act like little bitty babies, I would have never come over here! I was trying to show y'all how to be a woman but…"

Just then my mom burst into the room. "What's going on, in here??" I'm not a rat, so Donna and I just stared at Lisa waiting to see what she would say next.

Lisa smacked her lips and said, "Mrs. Johnson, my stomach is hurting. Can you take me home?"

Back at school on Monday, to say things were weird is an understatement. Everywhere I looked, someone was looking at me and whispering. Right before lunch, I always went to my locker to put my backpack inside so I wouldn't have to haul it through the cafeteria. Just as I closed my locker shut, there she was – Lisa. Not only Lisa but a whole bunch of people. I was so confused. Lisa smirked and said, "I heard you want to fight me?"

I chopped and screwed up my face and said, "Who told you that? I don't want to fight you, you're my friend."

The crowd erupted with laughter. I looked back and forth from the crowd to Lisa. Lisa said, "Nah, I said it, now what?"

Honestly, I was in pure shock! I couldn't process what was going on, let alone form a response to what Lisa was saying. Did Lisa think I would tell anyone what had happened? Is this what this was about? I would never tell on any of my friends. Loyalty meant everything to me. I guess I took too long to answer her, because the next thing I knew she slapped me. My emotions went from 0-60 real quick. Although I was hurt, the embarrassment and the audacity of the situation turned into pure anger. I ain't never been no punk, so I slapped that smirk off her face, and we went at it. We fought down the hall, outside to the recreation area and ended up along the side of the school's dumpster.

That's when she did it…She bit me!!

First, there was a stinging sensation, followed by what I assumed at the time was sweat pouring in my eye, clouding my vision. Then the pain; OMG, it felt like fire ants had attacked my eye. Taking both hands to cover my eye gave Lisa full advantage. It felt like an eternity as Lisa punched and swung and kicked until I felt…nothing. I looked up and through my blurred vision I saw Principal Henry dragging Lisa away.

Returning to school after my three-day suspension was embarrassing. I don't know if I was embarrassed because I didn't know what to expect the students to be saying about the fight, or if it was because of the big Texas sized bandage on the side of my eye to cover up the patch of skin that Lisa bit off my face! I learned to be careful about who I let in my house, because the other person may have a "licker" license.

3

First Boyfriend

The longest time my father stayed home was when my parents started a cleaning service, that did surprisingly well, and we were able to move to a new home. My new neighborhood was called Las Cimas. Our new home was a two-story home with four bedrooms, yellow siding on the sides, with a decent front yard and big back yard.

The only thing better than finally having my own room was my new high school. It was literally a five-minute walk from my house and the neighborhood school was Lit! L. B. J. High School was the most popular school in the city. Our purple and white Jaguar pride could be best described as pure SWAG. The football and track team were #1 in the city. L.B.J.'s band director was my first cousin, Quincy. They played hip hop songs during football games, so you know our games were "fire." But the thing that our school was most popular for was the best-looking females and the coolest guys.

I was super excited to see Donna on the first day of school. I saw her on my way to first period. She was walking toward me with a really friendly looking girl who was introduced to me as Tisha. She was shy and very smart. I liked her right away. We were like the three amigos, always together. I began to make other friends too. There was my mischievous friend named Rachel who lived down the street from me, and who was in three of my classes. Rachel was the one who helped me torment substitute teachers and beat up boys.

When we had a substitute teacher in class, it was over for them. Most of the time the substitute teacher would be fresh out of college – they were the ones that got it the worst! We would purposely disrupt the class, and then the sub would say, “Ladies, since you insist on talking, is there anything you would like to share with the class?” We would then explain that we weren’t learning anything and maybe they should seek another profession. The whole class would fall out laughing.

Rachel and I would beat up boys so bad that dudes would tense up and cover their chest when we came around, scared of a sudden blow to the chest or ribs. Boys never meant anything special to me. Unlike me, Rachel liked boys and even had a boyfriend, while I thought they were good to play sports or to just be plain ole punching bags.

High school days were the best. I’m sure in every school there was always a girl or a boy that was daring and appeared to just not care about the consequences. Well to me that was Brian; he was the craziest boy I’d ever met! He was short, stocky and bow-legged, with strong arms that reminded me of the cartoon character Popeye. He had what black folks back then called “good hair,” a mix between curly and wavy. He always wore it tapered short and neat. Brian had a way with words that left you shocked and confused, asking yourself, “Did he just say that?” He was real loud and could be heard before you even saw him. He would talk back to teachers and bullies – it didn't matter who you were!

I first noticed him when he was arguing with our star football quarter back, Jessie, over who could punch the hardest. Jessie towered over Brian, but Brian was heavier. Brian just walked up to Jessie and asked, "Let's see if I can knock you out before you knock me out."

Jessie looked confused but a crowd had already formed, and he didn't see a way out, so he went along with it.

Brian calmly walked right up to Jessie and punched him in the jaw, then stepped back and said, "Your turn!"

After Jessie recovered from shock, anger set in and he punched Brian in the face. This went on for about five minutes. Back and forth, punch after punch. The only reason it stopped was because they both got tired and fell to the ground. These two guys became the best of friends after that day.

I guess it was a respect thing.

Brian was the first boy who was not afraid of me and he would be the first boy to claim me as his "girlfriend." My first conversation with Brian was right after one of my volleyball games. He just walked up to me and said, "You're going to be my girlfriend."

"WHATEVER!" I retorted.

After that, I started hearing rumors going around that, "Nobody better be caught even speaking to Choc" because I belonged to Brian. I enjoyed the attention at first, so I went along with it. I put up with Brian because, when he was with me, he was gentle, caring, funny and protective, something I had never had before. But at base, I was afraid of him.

Brian had a bad habit of putting his hands on me. It started out when we would argue, and if I tried to walk away, he would yank my arm and tell me not to walk away from him while he was talking. Brian and I fought like cats and dogs. His controlling nature made me both mad and curious at the same time.

He has to really like me; that's why he's so passionate, right? I thought.

He would hold me down and put hickeys on my neck – it was his "mark" he would say. He would also say, "You know I love you, but you better not ever leave me."

Brian ended up getting kicked out of school and I wouldn't see him again until I was an adult. He would make good on his threat. At this season of my life, I learned that love doesn't hurt.

4

SMELLING MYSELF

I was a good student. I went to summer school every year for extra credit, so I was due to graduate at seventeen. By the time I was a senior, I only had three classes to graduate. My life was working out just like I planned, until I started smelling myself.

Yes, I turned into a normal sixteen-year-old teenager until my perception of boys started to change. I started noticing how fine they were and how good they smelled. I was also rebelling against my parents. I started losing respect for my mother and started distancing myself from her. I felt embarrassed for her; I felt she was weak because she kept taking my father back whenever he wanted to. I also started resenting my dad; his little disappearing acts had gotten old. I even stopped speaking to him because I was fed up with him leaving us.

I was also maturing physically. I had a nice pair of round, perky breasts, small waist, and nice country rear end, and country accent. For an early graduation present, my mother sent me to the dentist and surprised me with a gold tooth, with a heart in the middle that I put to my left side of the center rabbit teeth, just like Mary J. Blige.

My hobbies were dancing, class work, and beating up boys. And boy did I love old cars. At the age of sixteen I was the only one in the neighborhood with a car…a 1979 hunter green Monte Carlo trimmed in gold. My father had been working on this car for years and gave it to me probably also as a "gag order" gift to keep my mouth shut over who he was running around with all over town. Now that I was getting older, I was starting to hear things about my father's player ways.

We still had a cleaning service, so I saved my money and bought some used low profile rims, and a pull-out JVC deck with four 6 x 9 speakers. No one could tell me anything! Life was good!

I truly believe that everyone has a crossroad, and this was mine. I had another best friend whose name was Chauncey. She was older than me and she was a tall yellow girl with some of the biggest calves I'd ever seen. She was my "wise" friend; it seemed like anything I asked her about, she knew the answer. Ever since I disassociated myself from my mom, this was my "go to" person.

Still very much of a tomboy, I loved playing football and volleyball. On this particular day, I was playing kickball in front of Chauncey's house. I was wearing a pair of blue jean shorts and a red halter top that tied around my neck and back, holding the kickball. That's when I saw him! Just as Chauncey's little brother ran past me and headed for 3rd base, I couldn't move; it seemed like time stopped.

I could hear my team shouting "Hit him. Choc, hit him!" I guess all of the commotions made him look in my direction and that's when our eyes connected.

Todd wasn't much of a looker at first glance now that I think about it. He was a couple of years older than me. He dropped out of school in the eleventh grade to "hustle." He had what we call swag – his confidence was on ten. He had big eyes and small teeth, but his style was on point! He had on white Guess shorts and a red Guess Polo shirt and shoes to match. As he approached me, I could smell that Polo cologne.

"Dang, girl, you fine, can I get your number or what?" he said.

I came back to my senses when I heard Chauncey's voice yelling "Choc! Don't give that boy your number!"

Taking her advice, I put my hands on my hips and said, "When monkeys fly!"

Todd looked at me for a moment and burst out laughing. He said "Girl, where you from? I ain't never heard nobody talk like that before. You must be from the country."

I was so embarrassed, I threw the ball and yelled over my shoulder, "Chauncey, I'll see you later, girl," and went home.

Later that evening, Chauncey called me and said, "Uh, Choc, can you come over and help my little brother with his homework?" Instantly, I was aware that we were in "code." Something was up. I asked my mother if I could go to Chauncey's house to help her brother with his homework because we had the same class. That was a lie. By now I was barely speaking to my mom and probably to keep me on her good side she said, yes, since it was something pertaining to school.

I quickly pulled off my pajamas and put on some short shorts, midriff t-shirt and tennis shoes, and ran down the street at track star speed. I rang the doorbell and when Chauncey answered the door, she mouthed, "I'm sorry." I looked at her confused.

Instead of getting an ear full of some good ole gossip, my jaw nearly hit the floor. There he was again, Todd, but this time inside Chauncey's house. I looked at Chauncey and asked, "WTH is going on?" She just looked back with a sly grin and walked away.

I regained my composure and looked Todd up and down, "What do YOU want?" I said.

He walked over to me, gently grabbed my hand and walked me outside to the front porch. Todd took my face softly in his hands and kissed me. There on Chauncey's porch, I had my first kiss. When he kissed me, I literally melted into his arms. I don't know if it was because he held my hand – no man had ever held my hand before, not even my father. Or was it the way he caressed my face as he kissed me? I felt like silk – special.

From that day on, I guess you could say he was my boyfriend. He affectionately called me "Mama." He said it was because I acted old for my age. Todd was very protective and caring, unlike my father. He would walk about ten blocks to my house every day – rain, sleet or snow – just to sit and watch T.V. while my mother kept a close eye on us.

Todd and I talked about everything; he was my new best friend. I really liked spending time with him, in person or on the phone. I could count on him to be there. He was a father figure to me; he taught me a lot. He showed me how to wear clothes that accented my shape. He even had this real funny, flaming gay guy named Peaches teach me how to walk in high heels. Peaches was funny. He would march up to me with his short pixy cut, hair laid over one eye and ALL the colors in his outfits, snapping his big fingers, and saying, "Okay, Cookie, I'm gonna show you how to cook these heifers breakfast (snap), lunch (snap) and dinner (snap). When you walk on the scene, those cows gonna feel ill, okaaaaay, Miss Thang (clicking his tongue)?"

Todd could dress his butt off, so, of course, his lady had to be on point too. Todd sent me to the beauty shop to get my hair and nails done. We would get dressed in one of his "HOT" (booster) outfits that had not yet been on the department store racks yet, and show up fashionably late to a spot called Midtown on Cameron road and dance until the lights came on just because he knew I loved to dance.

Todd's greatest flaw was he was irresponsible. He loved the finer things in life and would get them by any means necessary. Since he dropped out of school in the 11th grade, he tried to work at restaurants, grocery stores, and places like that, but nothing panned out. His appetite for the fast money and his distaste for being "regular" would be his downfall. Anytime the streets would call, he would ALWAYS answer.

During the day, while I was at school or cleaning offices with my mom and sister, Todd would be out "getting his hustle on," as he would say. He would make fast money by stealing clothes from department stores and selling them to people for half the price tag. He would recruit people to go into a department store, preferably the mall, and right before closing time because there would always be one person to close the store. Someone would distract the sales person, and he would grab as many clothes as possible and put them in a "beeper bag," which would be placed inside a department store name bag that would prevent the alarm from going off, allowing him and his partner to walk smoothly out of the store. He would then sell the clothes for half of what was on the price tag.

When boosting clothes was slow, he would dabble in selling drugs. He wasn't too good at it, because each time he tried, after only a few days he would get caught and get taken to jail. I stuck by him though and stayed loyal. I accepted and paid for collect phone calls with my cleaning service money and would visit him in jail on the weekend. I was turning into an addict myself, living by the street code, the attention, the money! I became addicted to "The Life."

Thankfully, Todd was not locked up for my senior prom. It was finally my big night at the Omni Hotel in downtown Austin. So, you KNOW, Peaches hooked us up! The ballroom was decorated like an elegant fairy tale. I made my entrance wearing a lace long sleeved, royal blue, mermaid bateau illusion form fitting dress, silver accessories, with a pair of six-inch black Christian Louboutin heels and a silver tierra neatly placed on my head. By my side, Todd was wearing a white Tom Ford Windsor suit with a royal blue tie and blue and silver faux leather loafers. All night, Todd could not keep his eyes or hands off of me. Our energy was electric. While slow dancing, Todd whispered in my ear, "May I have you tonight, Mama?"

I nervously answered, "Yes."

Todd always knew a person that knew a person, so getting us a room at this expensive hotel was no problem. As soon as we entered the room, Todd wasted no time in unzipping my dress, kissing me everywhere! My mind was overwhelmed with mixed thoughts of happiness and being afraid of the expectation of this magical moment into womanhood. I thought back when Lisa from middle school said that the feeling would be indescribable pleasure. I thought about the many movies that I had watched, where the girl would see stars! As he laid me down my mind was screaming, "This is it! I'm about to lose my virginity!!" Todd was very loving, very patient, very considerate and, and…and very quick. Yep, after about five minutes of pure torture, I lay there listening to him snore, thinking, where are the stars, where is this magical moment that is supposed to happen? WOW!

Now I know why they say you "lose" your virginity.

Graduation day was super lit, but sad at the same time. I looked around and knew some of the faces I saw that day, I probably would never see again. Later on that night, Todd was over eating dinner with my mom and sister. Yep, you guessed it, my father decided not to show up for that either. I announced that I would be going to the military in four months…more for my sister and Todd because my mom had taken me down to take the test and swear in a couple of weeks later. I could not get in until I turned 18. The way Todd had been in and out of jail, I thought he would be happy for me. My plan was to go to the military and when I came home, Todd and I would get married and get our own place and not have to depend on his "hustle."

But, much to my surprise, Todd excused himself from the table and walked out the door. Wow!

My hood threw me a slamming going away party. A few people I kicked it with at school came by too. We partied until the sun came up.

The day I left for the military to "be all that I could be," Todd never showed up. My father did not show up either. I cried all the way to the bus station. I was sad because I had not seen or heard from him since the night he just walked out. He didn't answer my phone calls and wasn't at his usual hang-out spots. I was upset because he didn't give me a chance to explain – how I was doing this for us.

Everyone was quiet on the bus ride to Lackland Air Force Base in San Antonio, nervous for what was in store. As we got closer, I was up for the challenge. I had packed darn near everything I owned in my suitcase when I went to basic training with plans on never returning. I didn't know what to look forward to, but I did know I was accustomed to looking cute. I had on this kayuuuuuute little outfit that Peaches hooked me up with. I was looking good if I do say so myself. As soon as we got off the bus, everyone was told to line up in formation, look forward, put the suitcases down, shut up and listen.

A big muscular white man in uniform with a big rim hat and big shiny boots, sounding like tap shoes, started shouting something about we now belonged to Uncle Sam that there would be no more crying to mommy and daddy. *Who the heck is Uncle Sam?* I thought.

The drill sergeant shouted, "Pick up your bags! Now put them down! Now pick them back up!"

Well round about the tenth time of him saying this, you know ya girl had had enough. I was tired and my suitcase was too dang heavy for this foolishness. I raised my hand and said, "Uh, excuse me, Sir, do you want us to put them up or down?"

Big mistake. All eyes were on me. Mr. Big Hat walked up to me with those metal plates underneath his shoes making each step echo off the walls. He leaned in and yelled in my face, saying I could not speak, eat or poop unless he told me to. I tried to explain to him that my bag was heavy, and I was tired and plus I had to pee. But before I could get one word out, he told me to follow him. He had something for me to do.

Oh, I was able to use the latrine – aka the restroom – but then I was given a change of clothes, from my fashionable cute outfit to a pair of oversized BDUs (Basic Military Uniform) and a trash bag. *Now why would I need a trash bag*? I thought. He told me to pick up every leaf off this courtyard until there wasn't a leaf left. It was the middle of October and there were leaves blowing everywhere. Three trash bags later, I was finally relieved from duty at 1:00 a.m. (0100 hours), not knowing that "Reveille," a trumpet call used to wake military personnel all over the base, was at 3:00 a.m. (0300 hours).

Eventually, I got the hang of things and learned to keep my mouth shut and just do what I was told. It made things much easier. All the same, years of me being a tomboy paid off. Every morning at 0300 we ran three miles, did 100 sit-ups and 100 push-ups. Then we'd go back to the dorms, take a shower and hike a mile to the chow hall for breakfast. We would go to class in the afternoons or complete a physical confidence course. The physical confidence courses were my favorite! I was killing the obstacle courses, and almost made marksmanship in shooting at moving targets. I was so rough in the self-defense course that they had to get a man to spar with me.

I even got a chance to lead the cadence while marching a few times! HUT, TWO, THREE, FOUR!

I successfully graduated from Basic Training and was sent to Biloxi, Mississippi to Technical Training School to prepare me for my next assignment. Once I got there, a tall slim man in uniform approached me. When he walked up to me, he introduced himself by his last name like everyone in the military did. He said, "I am Sergeant Smith and I will be your guide. Go get settled in and report to the chow hall at 14:30."

"Yes, Sir," I replied, and then I reported as ordered.

We met every day at the chow hall at the same time. He would show me where my classes were and walk me to the military store to buy things that I needed. He even purchased some things for me. On our third meeting, he revealed to me that he was not a guide at all. He started this charade because he was trying to impress me. But, the more that he got to know me, the more he started to have strong feelings for me. We hung out and went to dinner a couple of times, but I told him that I didn't want to lead him on and that my heart still belonged to Todd.

I lost about thirty pounds from all that training, bringing me to a whopping ninety pounds!

I graduated with honors! I got lucky and was stationed right outside of Austin. My job was that of legal assistant and I loved it. The base was 30 minutes away from my parents' home in Austin, so I was able to go home every day.

When I went home, things were changing in a sense, yet still the same. Papa was still a rolling stone. My mother was still unsure about what she was doing wrong to make him keep leaving her. But now she had friends that she hung out with; she was even on a soft ball team! My sister was off to college at Prairie View University. She even joined a sorority, Alpha Phi Zeta. I was proud of her. It seemed like she was finally coming out of her shell and at a place in her life where she felt comfortable.

However, Todd was a completely different story. He had become very showy, wearing a lot of jewelry, and he was always flashing his money. Todd apparently had a new best friend, Stan. Stan was 6'4, 200 pounds and very quiet; he would always nod his head in acknowledgment whenever he saw me.

Todd never spoke to me about the type of hustling he was doing. But one day, when I came home from work, I was surprised to see Todd sitting in front of my house in a drop top, baby blue C Class Benz. Although outwardly I was smiling and congratulating him, secretly I was scared and concerned that Todd was in too deep. While I was away in basic training, Todd, Stan and Stan's girlfriend, Carla, had moved in together to a house on the Eastside near downtown. Stan was reserved, but Carla and I hit it off instantly. Carla talked really fast and always kept me laughing. Stan and Carla had an adorable one-year old little girl. That made me wonder what our child would look like.

###

I was thriving in my career, so much so that I was told by Major Willis that I would be promoted from Airman to Sergeant. I called my mom and sister and told them the good news. But I decided that I would take off early and go celebrate with my baby Todd – besides, he always told me how good I looked to him in my uniform.

As I pulled up to Carla's house, I noticed Todd's Benz was parked in the driveway. I got out and knocked on the door. Carla answered and said, "Ooh, girl, you look cute!" She nervously looked over her shoulder and said, "I thought you were coming by later this evening?"

I told her, "Yeah, but I couldn't wait to tell my baby I got promoted today!"

She looked at me sympathetically, looked back inside then back to me. "Todd! Choc is here," she announced.

I walked in and headed to Todd's room. As I got closer, I heard voices and shuffling. When I opened the door, there, sitting on the bed, was a young dark-skinned girl, putting on her shirt. She looked to be around seventeen years old. Her face was beat for the gods; she had full pouty lips painted red, really long fake eyelashes and designer long nails. She kept her eyes on Todd. I turned to look at Todd for answers. He couldn't even look at me. I watched him with no shirt on, fumbling with the zipper on his pants. He said, "Uh, hey, Mama, I thought you were coming by later?"

To say I was hurt was an understatement; I was distraught! I didn't say a word. I just turned around and walked out of the room. As I passed the living room in a blur; I heard Carla say, "Choc! Choc! Are you okay?"

I walked out of the house and didn't even bother to close the door. I would never be the same again.

I channeled my anger and hurt energy into my work, a coping mechanism that I saw my mother use each time my father left. It helped numb some of the pain. I even signed up for classes at Austin Community College. If I wasn't at work or school, I was sleeping.

The only person that I could talk to was Chauncey; I told her what happened, and she tried to comfort me. She kept reminding me that I had a promising future and I needed to find someone else. But I couldn't see past wanting him. After weeks of Chauncey trying to talk some sense into me, I finally persuaded her to help me find him and get some answers.

We were finally able to catch up with him. Chauncey's cousin told her he hung out at one of the roughest places in East Austin, 12th street, a place we called "the cuts," where you could find drug dealers, crack heads, people gambling, and street walkers all hours of the day and night. Chauncey and I were deathly afraid of the cuts, but to help me get the answers I needed, Chauncey was there for me. When we spotted him, he was leaning against a 78 primer Cutlass, flirting with females. He even hit a chick on her butt as she walked by. I had never seen this Todd before. All I could do was stare.

I must have been starring hard because just then a guy stood next to me and said, "You can do better."

I turned toward the voice and all I could say was, "Dang!"

He stood about 6-foot, skin the color of butterscotch, looking at me licking his lips looking like L.L. Cool J. He followed my eyes and said it again, "You can do better," bringing my attention back to Todd.

He wanted to know why someone as pretty as me would be worried about someone like Todd. This made me smile and got my attention because I didn't have an answer. He reached out his hand and introduced himself.

"Hey, pretty lady, my name is Chris."

I winked my eye at Chauncey, letting her know the code for *I got a potential prospect on the hook*. Although she wanted to protest, she had not seen me smile in a while and, seeing where we were, she just said, "I'll be in the car."

Chris and I followed, slowly walking towards my car, I was attracted to Chris's no-nonsense exterior. He was soft spoken, but straightforward. He reminded me of Ice Cube. When we arrived at my car, Chauncey was talking to her cousin Shay who lived right down the street from where we were – that's how she knew where Todd hung out. Chris and I got in my backseat for a little privacy. I ain't going to lie. The game he was spitting was just what I needed to hear. He was laying it on thick, saying things like if he had a girl like me, there is no way that he would ever cheat on her.

Suddenly, the car door was pulled open. There he was – Todd! He was looking dead at me with a mixture of hurt and confusion. Regaining his composer, Todd lifted his chin up, sniffed and said, "Mama, let me holla at you for a second."

I told him to go back over there and "holla" at those other girls!"

Chris interjected, "Ay, player, I don't think she wants to talk to you, so you can close the door."

They started arguing, so to prevent them from attracting unnecessary attention, I told Chris, "Can you give me five minutes, please." Chris squinted his eyes, smiled and nodded his head in approval.

As soon as I got out the car, Todd began to "apolo-lie" and tell me how I had it all wrong, that the girl I saw in the room was trying on clothes to buy. He began telling me he missed me and was willing to do whatever it took to get me back. I began to soften up because I really wanted it to work for us. I don't know how Todd took my silence, but all of a sudden, he started yelling at me.

"I can't believe you're in the car with that dude! You'd better not get back in that car with him!" A crowd was starting to form.

Chris got out of the car and told me, "Don't even waste your breath on him. Drop that zero and get with this hero!"

Todd grabbed me close to him and told Chris, "THIS IS MY WOMAN!"

Chris said, "If she your woman, why was she about to leave with me?"

Before I knew it, Todd ran toward Chris and hit Chris in the face. Everything got crazy. People were pushing one way to see the fight. Chauncey and I were running from it, trying to get away. That's when I saw Stan, standing on the top of a car. He pulled out his gun and started shooting it in the air! People started running and yelling, and Chauncey and I ran with Shay to her house for safety.

Once Shay let us know that the coast was clear and the crowd returned back to normal, I asked Chauncey if she was ready. She was pissed! She said, "I can't believe I let you talk me into coming here!" I felt ashamed; she had every right to blame me. "We could have gotten hurt out there tonight! All because you just HAD to see Todd!" she yelled.

Chauncey was so mad, she stayed with Shay. I started walking to my car alone. As I approached the car, I was surprised to see Chris leaning against my car. He was covered with scratches and bruises all over his face and his lip was still bleeding. He turned to me and asked me whether I was ready to go get something to eat, as if nothing had happened. I felt horrible that Chris had a fight over me. Since it was all my fault, I said, "Sure."

I got in the driver's seat and, as soon as I closed my door, I felt something cold and sharp on my neck. I could feel Chris' breath in my ear saying, "If I ever see you with that nigga again, I will kill you! Do you understand?"

I nodded my head in submission.

I was so afraid that Chris would make good on his threat that I continued to see him for a while. It turns out that Chris sold drugs, too. He was Todd's competition. Sadly, Chris had a habit of sampling his own supply. A few weeks after the fight, we were hanging out at his house. I watched him smoke weed and, to my surprise, he dipped it in PCP. He changed right there before my eyes. He went from telling me I was a beautiful chocolate lady to yelling at me, saying he was going to put a baby in me – that way I couldn't leave him!

I slowly but surely drifted away from Chris, blaming it on work or school. After a while he was so caught up in selling and using drugs he didn't even notice.

###

I slowly started to enjoy life again, now as a single woman. Since my favorite thing was dancing, I always ended up at the clubs. I wouldn't call it dating, but I went through a period of just having fun. Old people would call it "being fast." My first quest was a guy name Shawn. Shawn was the little brother of my good friend and classmate Shaunie. If Shaunie ever found out about Shawn and me, she would have killed me! Shawn had been crushing on me forever and Shaunie would always say, “Choco, you’d better not mess with my brother!”

Shawn was quiet, almost shy acting, and always smiling. He was a little taller than me. When he looked at me, it reminded me of the singer Prince, like he wanted to do something to me. Just like Prince, Shawn was a pure freak and I loved that we kept our freaky-deakie on the low, just between us.

When we first hooked up Shawn bought me this cute purple pager. We had a favorite hotel that we would go to, but whenever we saw one another at the club, we would never interact. When I received the page “325,” which was our favorite room at the hotel, it was on and popping!

Whenever he brought a snickers bar and orange juice, I’d know I was in for a long night! We would go at it all…night…long!

Shawn was young but he had his head on straight and he was not only book smart, but he was street wise too. He knew what he wanted out of life and didn’t just talk about it; he made his dreams a reality. That was my young Bae.

5

FOREVER CHANGED

One night at a new popular club, there he was again, Brian. Yes, he was still bullying me, saying it was like the mafia to release his hold over his girl. I had just walked in the club and wanted to enjoy my night. I didn't want to get into it with him, so I had to think of something fast. I knew I was treading on thin ice. Brian had seen me out with Shawn a couple of times, and I knew he was angry with me. Although he and I had not been together since high school, he would often remind me that I would ALWAYS be his.

So, I walked up to him first and hugged him, told him he looked nice tonight, and tried to butter him up. I told him I missed him and asked the whereabouts of his sister Karen. He didn't say anything at first; he just looked at me suspiciously. Nervously, I told him a lie about why I was looking for her.

To keep him distracted and confused, I asked him, "What do you think about me taking your little sister out with me to Midtown? You know I'll take care of her."

He knew his little sister Karen always wanted to hang out, but he would only let her go out with people he trusted. His suspicion turned into happiness when I mentioned that I would even come to their house and pick her up. He said, "Alright, but make sure you be there. Don't make me come looking for you, baby." He slapped me on my butt and walked off.

I knew Brian told his sister what I said, because the next day she was blowing me up trying to coordinate what we were going to wear later that night for Women's Night. I was surprised that her parents were going to let her go out on a weekday and asked what they said. She said her parents were out of town, but Brian said it was cool.

Later that evening, I started getting ready. By now it was a given that I was going to be one of the sharpest sisters at the club. So about eight o'clock, I jumped in the shower, got out and dabbed my skin dry with a towel. I moisturized my entire body with cocoa butter lotion. I put on a little concealer, mascara and lip gloss. I rocked this bad hunter green mini skirt outfit, with rhinestones along the base of the skirt and a black hat with rhinestones on the brim to match. The skirt was fitting kind of tight so, of course, that meant I had to rock a black G-String so I would not have any panty lines. I slipped on my favorite pair of six-inch black wide heels that tied around my ankles. They allowed me to do my best catwalk that could stop traffic, thanks to Peaches!

As soon as I drove up to Brian's parent's house, I felt weird, a little hesitant, about going into their house without their parents being home. I thought about blowing the horn to let Karen know I was outside but, knowing Brian, he wouldn't let us go until he harassed me about Shawn – which is really why he was letting his sister go in the first place. Brian would make a big deal and probably wouldn't let her go. Karen had been planning all day and I didn't want her to be disappointed. As I walked to the door, I was thinking of ways that I could flatter Brian so we could hurry and leave. I had to get my nerves together because, I was low key scared of what he had in store for me after seeing me out with Shawn.

Like dogs, men can smell fear and use it to their advantage and Brian was a Rottweiler! I knocked on the door; thankfully, Karen answered and invited me inside; she mentioned that she would be ready in 10 minutes. "Oh, Brian is in his room and wants to talk to yooou," she sang.

Oh man! Here we go! Let's get this over with. I slowly walked towards the back of the house to the room that had the light on. I knocked lightly, and heard Brian say, "Come in!" He was lying down on his weight bench lifting weights. I walked in and stood over him, while he pushed the weights in the air, but never taking his eyes off me.

He said, "About time, I thought I was going to have to go looking for you tonight." Brian loved giving me a hard time; he said it was because I looked so cute when I was angry. He started up with his usual fatherly probing questions:

Brian: Where are y'all going?

Me: Midtown

Brian: What time will y'all be back?

Me: I'll have Karen back by midnight if we can ever hurry up and leave!

Brian: (sitting up on the bench) Then, where are you going, to see Shawn?

The look on his face switched so suddenly that I laughed nervously trying to figure out how to respond. That must have pissed him off; he jumped up and slammed the door and locked it.

He pushed me down on the bed, grabbed my keys and threw them; they landed at the top of his closet where his hats were lined up. He walked back to me so close our noses touched and said, "Now I'm going to ask you again."

I had to think fast, in hopes of getting my keys back. I seductively licked his lips and ran my hand over the back of his head and kissed him. I said, "Baby, now you know I don't want no one but you. Now stop being mean to me and give me my keys; I bet Karen is waiting on me to go."

Ever since we dated in high school, we had a routine, which would go something like this: he would take something of mine, run off or hide it. He would tell me the only way to get it back would be to give him a kiss. We would kiss and he would give it back. We'd been doing this for years!

But this time was different: he grabbed me and kissed me hard. He was hurting me. When I pushed him away, he slapped me! I couldn't believe he just hit me! I was trying to play it cool and didn't fight him at first because I didn't want to get him more upset. But the look in his eyes was scaring me. He pinned my hands above my head and took a jump rope that was hanging on the headboard and tied my wrists together. I tried to kick him but, he put all of his weight on me so I couldn't kick or even close my legs. He started kissing my face and my neck; he raised up my shirt and kissed my breasts and moved down toward my private.

I was shocked at first, and kept saying over and over, "STOP BRIAN, I've got to go!"

I tried to free my hands, but the rope was so tight it started burning into my skin. I tried to fight him off, but he was too strong. He grabbed one of my legs with one hand and ripped my G string off. While Brian took over my body, my mind escaped.

Sure, I'd seen ladies on T.V. late at night running in the park, getting raped by a complete stranger! So, this couldn't be rape...right? I knew Brian. We dated in high school and I thought he cared about me, even loved me – at least that was what he kept saying over and over in my ear. Maybe I was tripping, maybe this is his way of showing me he loved me. We have a history; Brian wouldn't hurt me...right?

If I told someone, would they say, "That's what she gets for wearing that short skirt over there when the parents were away!"

"What would Todd say? Where is my father? I thought fathers protected their daughters. Where the HECK is Karen? OMG did Karen set this up? Does she know what her brother is doing to me? Does she care?" I asked myself.

I could hear Brian in the background during all of my thinking, breathing heavily in my ear, saying, "This is mine, you hear me?" I figured out really quick that the more I fought, the more Brian would be aroused, and the more painful it would be for me. So, I just laid there, praying that he would hurry up and finish. I just wanted to go home. I was so detached, I didn't even feel him get up and leave the room, until I felt a warm wash towel between my legs. You would have thought we'd made passionate love the way he gently took his time and washed me off from my neck down to my toes. But he never looked me in the eye. He picked my clothes up and handed them to me and left the room. As soon as the door closed, I quickly put them on.

Now what?

He must have felt guilty or scared. All night he tried to explain over and over how I made him do it. "Choc, you know I love you. What did you think would happen coming to my house looking all good?" He said he just couldn't control himself. I'm not sure if Brian tried to comfort me or justify himself. During the night he just held me and asked me if I felt cold, then covered me with a blanket; he kept kissing my face and telling me he loved me.

He must have been afraid that I would call the police because he did not let me go home until 6:00 a.m. I don't remember leaving his house, or even driving home. What I do remember is going straight to the shower and scrubbing my skin so hard, thinking that, maybe, if I scrubbed hard enough, I could make it un-happen! Maybe it didn't happen; maybe I dreamed it! But as I scrubbed, flashes of the night crossed my mind!

I dried off, my skin still tingling.

As I was leaving the restroom, I bumped right into my father! Before I could say a word, he yelled, "You think you're grown?! He continued, "I don't care how old you are. If you are going to live here, you will be in this house at a decent time!"

I just stared at him, thinking to myself, "How does he not know that I'm hurting?? Does he care?" He turned and walked away.

It would take me years to come to terms with what Brian did to me. There was not as much information about date rape back then. I spent a lot of energy blaming myself. But it changed me to the core. I was angry, angry with myself for going over there. I was angry with Karen because I think she set me up. I was angry with Todd for hurting me and not being there to protect me. I was angry that I couldn't tell my dad. When I was alone, I prayed a lot but, mostly, I cried and tried not to think about it. Over time I blocked it out.

Still scarred, still hurt, I've never told a soul about that night until now.

Todd and I tried a few times to rekindle what we had; we were not successful. However, we did successfully become pregnant with a beautiful baby girl named Rhiannon, that means Great Queen. I knew she was going to be special in the way she came into the world.

That morning I awoke with a jerk, then another one. I ran to the restroom, thinking I had to use the toilet. As I wiped myself there was blood. Umph, am I supposed to be bleeding? Ouch, there it goes again, that sharp pain! I called out to my mother and showed her the blood. Her eyes got as big as saucers.

"It's time!" she shouted, possibly the ONLY time my father and mother were there for me at the same time. They rushed me to the hospital. My father dropped my mom and me at the entrance of the emergency room and burned rubber to go park. As soon as I stepped one foot into the hospital, I felt a gush of water come from between my legs. I fell to the ground in pain and embarrassment.

My mother flagged down a man in blue scrubs and shouted, "We need help! The baby is coming!"

He casually walked over to me and said, "She'll be okay; she still has time. Let me get you a stretcher."

As soon as he walked away, a pain came over my whole body that made me push. And just that quickly, I heard my mom yelling, "I got the baby; I got the baby!" So, there on the floor of the entrance of the emergency room, my mom delivered my baby girl! I named Chauncey the godmother.

After delivering Rhiannon, my mother and daughter developed a bond that I couldn't compete with. Rhiannon also saved my mother's life by giving her the strength to finally confront and divorce my father.

6

MARRIED LIFE

Anytime you saw me after that I was alone. That was until I met Diamond, yes, her real name is Diamond. I met Diamond at a popular club called Phases in Austin, Texas. I'd noticed her before at other clubs. She had a reputation of fighting, not only fighting but knocking women out! She was a triple threat, 5'7, light skinned and bow-legged. But what stood out for me was her confidence. It demanded respect.

Every time, I saw her she was dressed up, hair done and looking flawless. This particular time, I walked into the club looking like chocolate Haagen-Daz ice cream. Peaches was still hooking me up with that five-finger discount, so you know I was fresh to death. I had a two-drink minimum, so I made my way to the bar, when someone hit my shoulder so hard that I spun around a whole 360. As I grabbed the bar to catch my fall, I scuffed my black Christian Louboutin's! I was vexed! I turned around and yelled "Damn, you need to watch where you're going!"

That's when I met the ugliest woman this side of creation. She was 6' ft tall, had the face of a wildebeest, hair slicked down with way too much grease. But what made my butt pucker was when she bent down. So, we were face to face and she asked me, "What did you say little bitty girl?"

Now I ain't and never been no punk, but Mama didn't raise no fool either. I lowered my voice and said, "All I was saying was, you could at least say, excuse me."

"And if I don't?" she responded, pushing me.

She gave me no choice! I hit her in her face as hard as I could! Once the bouncers pulled us apart, I could hear someone yelling, "Now that's how you do it!" It was Diamond. "That little chocolate girl handled her business; she stood up to that big gorilla!"

My lip was busted, and my shoes were through. But I was so excited that Diamond, someone whom I admired, was proud of me that I didn't even care. After that, when you saw her, you saw me. We were inseparable; she was my ride or die. The only time we were apart was when Diamond went out of town. She would beg me to go out of town and I would always decline.

One day Diamond called me and said, "Girl, I've got the perfect guy for you!"

Reluctantly, I gave her the go-ahead to give him my number.

Surprisingly, Cameron and I hit it off instantly. Diamond was right; he seemed perfect. After a couple of weeks of talking on the phone, I rode with Diamond to Dallas to meet Cameron in person. We met at a club and I was pleasantly surprised. Cameron was 6'2, bald headed and his skin was paper sack brown. He was a firefighter and was about his business. He drove a black and gold Cherokee jeep and owned a home in a gated community.

We danced and talked all night long. As Cameron and I were getting closer and closer, Diamond and I began to drift apart. After a short courtship, Cameron asked me to marry him and I gladly said yes! With just Cameron, my mom and my pastor at my church, I became Mrs. Johnson.

We moved to Killeen, Texas so I would not have a long commute to work from Austin. I would work Monday-Thursday and go home Friday, Saturday and Sunday.

One Thursday night Diamond called me and asked if she could stay at my house in the spare room so she could go to ladies' night at the NCO club. Jokingly, I laughed and said, "Hell naw, I don't let no woman be at my house unless I am there."

She didn't laugh and said, "Oh, okay, that's fine."

A few months later I picked up the phone to call Diamond and, as if on cue, the phone rang. I wanted to ask her to be the godmother and tell her that I was at the hospital. I had just given birth to a fat, curly haired baby boy named Endubis, after a powerful African king. He was so long and had this intense stare to the point where it was creepy. I explained to Diamond that at one point I had to ask the nurse to switch him to the other side of the bed because he was just staring at me. But, lo and behold, he just slowly turned his head the other way and continued to stare. He was for sure going to be a mama's boy.

I was cracking up – until I noticed that Diamond wasn't laughing. In fact, I think she was crying. "What's wrong?" I asked.

Slowly, she began to explain to me that on the night she asked me if she could stay over my house and I told her, no, she stayed anyway and, as she put it, Cameron and she kind of messed around. It felt like she stabbed me in the heart. Betrayal from a friend is the worst. Hurts like hell.

Cameron and I stayed together, determined to work on our marriage because of the kids. We agreed to get away and move to Florida. My coworkers decided to throw us a party at Midtown a few days before we left. Cameron dropped me off at the door of Midtown so he could go park the car. As soon as he drove off, I turned around – and there he was…Brian.

Before I knew it, Brian had picked me up and taken me next door to an apartment complex hallway. I tried not to bring attention to us. But once he put me down, I started swinging. A security officer walked up to me. Since I didn't want Cameron to get involved with Brian, I immediately started explaining to the security officer that I was being held against my will and my husband was looking for me. The security officer told me to leave, but Brian grabbed my hand and told the security guard to mind his own business. The security and Brian ended up arguing; then a full out fight followed. I took that opportunity to slip back in the club without Cameron ever knowing what had happened.

The first two years living in Florida were marital bliss. Cameron worked a lot; so, we made sure to have date night every week. Then all of a sudden, he explained that he would be going out of town to training. The "training" became more frequent.

I'd met a few people by now who started feeling sorry for me and helped me out. My neighbor Stephanie would take me to the store when Cameron was away "training." My other neighbor Michelle and I helped each other out also. Michelle was a schoolteacher – a pretty yellow bone with "good" hair. She had a great personality and was a teacher at the local elementary school. She would watch the kids for me when I needed to go somewhere, and I would ride with her to catch her "dudes" when he was somewhere, he was not supposed to be.

I remember once Michelle got us some concert tickets to see two well-known artists. One of them was an R & B singer and the other one was a rapper from back in the day. She was in love with the singer and I was and still am in love with rapper to this day. The concert was amazing!! When the rapper was performing, I wormed my way to the stage. I must have looked star struck because he bent down and handed me a rose. It was plastic, but that's not the point. The point is as he was handing it to me, of all people, the rose. Then, all of a sudden, this little white girl grabs my rose! My eyes must have told the rapper what was about to happen because he, with his buttery skin and luscious lips, got my attention by touching my chin and handing me another plastic rose. I died and went to heaven!

The tickets allowed us to go backstage. We mistakenly got into the wrong line, not aware that there were two lines, one for the singer and one for the rapper. We were escorted into the singer's room and asked to dump our purses and have a seat. I wasn't dumping nothing, plus I was salty that I wasn't going to meet my "Baby daddy" the rapper. Since I wouldn't give the bouncers my purse, he said I couldn't go in the back. That was fine with me. I told Michelle to go ahead; it was her ticket in the first place.

As I sat in the lobby, I watched young girls walk in to meet the singer. I didn't think anything of it until I saw that same little white girl that took my rose come out of one the rooms in her bra and panties. She was leaning on the singer as he was smoking weed. I heard him say, "If you not fucking me, take your tired stank-ass home." As he walked towards me, I could instantly smell the weed mixed with sweat. He asked me why I was sitting in the lobby and not inside. I explained to him that I had gotten in the wrong line and I didn't want to dump my purse. He said, "Do you know who I am?"

I said, "Yes, sir."

He said, "So you don't want to meet me?"

I started to explain to him that Michelle was inside, and she was a really big fan of his, but he cut me off and told me to "get the fuck out." Tuh, no problem. I politely went out into the hallway.

Not even one minute later, Michelle came running out with her three top buttons missing. With tears in her eyes, she said, "LET'S GO! LET'S GO!" Literally, in between crying all the way home, she explained that the singer was having sex with young girls and tried to take advantage of her, too.

###

My marriage slowly declined to the point where we hardly saw one another. My husband would "train" during the year and I would take the kids to Tennessee in June to spend time with his family for a month, and then to Austin in July to spend time with my side of the family.

I remember it like it was yesterday. I was in Austin and got a call from Michelle telling me that a girl that she went to school with just went into my house with an overnight bag. I called and called and called the house, but Cameron never answered. I left a long voicemail. He ended up calling me back late that night.

I asked about the mystery chick and he just kept saying, "What girl? I don't know what you're talking about."

I decided to cut my trip short and fly back to Florida that next morning. When I arrived home, Cameron wasn't there, so I decided to go over and get the details from Michelle. Michelle repeated what she'd told me and added, "She works right up the street at the courthouse and her name is Eve."

I went home, got dressed up and headed to the courthouse. The county that we lived on was fairly small. There were two black women working behind the desk. But only one fit the description that Michelle gave me. The room was set up like a bank, so I got in line between the two velvet maroon ropes and waited until the next window was available. As I got closer to the front of the line, our eyes locked. I read her name badge; she gave me a faint smile and sort of cocked her head as if she was trying to remember where she had seen me before. I wanted to scream, "Maybe all of the pictures in my home, you Slut!"

When it was my turn, the other black lady said, "May I help you?" I pointed my finger at Eve and said, "I want 'her' to help me." All of her coworkers started looking at her as she nervously dropped some paper and pens to the floor. I guess she'd figured out who I was. I walked up to her window and just stared at her. She was pretty, light skinned (I thought Cameron said he only dated dark-skinned women); she wore contacts and was rail thin! Interrupting my thoughts, she said, "May I help you?"

I smiled my biggest smile and spoke as loud as I could. "Yes, what paperwork would you file if you know that someone that works here is cheating with a married man?" All of the blood left her face and you could hear a pin drop. I think even the printer and fax machine stopped.

She leaned in and asked, "Can I talk to you outside?"

I said, "Did you want to talk to me before you slept with my husband in my house?" She was so embarrassed that she took off through the employee entrance behind the glass. When I finally made it back through the line, she was gone!

I drove Michelle's car back and told her the whole story as she rolled all over the floor laughing so hard she cried. When I made it home the phone was ringing. I answered.

Cameron yelled, "Why did you go to that girl's job?"

To which I replied, "What girl?"

Needless to say, that marriage was done!!

I filed for divorce and moved back to Austin, Texas where my mother gladly welcomed us.

GUYS WILL BE GUYS

I dated this younger guy named Quinton. He was a huge guy standing at 6'4 and 245 lbs. of pure muscle. We met at the grocery store as he was stocking shelves. He would chase the kids and give them pieces of gum every time we came there. Eventually, he asked if he could take us all out to eat. To me that was impressive because he wanted to spend time with not just me, but all of us as a package.

We started doing everything together, going to the park, grocery shopping and even church. We did everything just like a family. He would come over with bags of groceries and fix up meals that could feed ten people. After a year, he proposed, and I accepted. We had a pretty consistent routine that ensured he would be at my apartment every day. So, one day when he did not come over, I didn't think anything about it at first – until that one day became three days. Even the kids were questioning where he was.

We drove by his house and his car was not there. He brought us by his father's house to introduce us when he proposed so I thought that I'd go by there and see if he knew where he was.

To my surprise, his father told me he was in jail, but he did not know why. The next day I took off work, took the kids to daycare and headed to the jail house. I waited for about three hours before a detective came out and talked to me. He told me that Quinton was in jail for attempted rape! He even let me read the witness' statement:

> *My name is Sherie; the below statement is true to my knowledge.*
>
> *At a work gathering at Crabs Seashack, Quinton became sick, I assume because he drank too much on an empty stomach because the food had not been served yet. He went to the restroom and after about an hour and forty-five minutes he came stumbling out. By then, most of the staff had left and gone home. There was only me and Shawn there waiting to make sure Quinton was okay. Shawn asked him if he was okay and did he need a ride home. Quinton told him, no; he would just go to his truck and sleep it off. Since Shawn left, I grabbed Quinton around the waist to hold him up and he draped his arm around my shoulder. It took us a while to get to the truck because he was so heavy, and he had parked at the back of the restaurant. Once we got to the truck, I took his keys and pressed the button to open the door. As soon as I opened the door, he grabbed me and laid me over the seat. He held both of my wrists together with one hand and lifted my dress and pulled at my panties until they ripped apart. He was slurring in my ear that I smelled good and he knew I wanted him. I screamed at him to stop, but he wouldn't let my wrists go! A car's headlights flashed on us as it*

was going by and, as if being woken from a trance, he opened his eyes real big and let me go.

I couldn't believe it! But at that moment I made a decision that I will not risk my kids around him.

###

I moved to Houston and four years later, I finished my degree in criminal justice and started working as a juvenile supervision officer. I attended church regularly and even became a Life Coach through Tony Gaskins Academy. My kids were adjusting to school and spending time with their biological dads. All that was missing was someone to share my life with.

Professionally, my life was flourishing. I was working with the Justice Department. I had just been promoted to supervisor working as a juvenile officer. I owned a home in Houston, Texas, and drove a two-door black Mercedes coupe. My profession kept me physically fit. Although I had accomplished these things, life is nothing unless you have someone to share it with. Having a strong relationship with God, I understood that being in a strong, loving relationship is very important for emotional stability. I wanted someone to love and support me.

A friend of mine told me about a dating app, and after much hesitation, I decided to make a profile, very careful not to put in too much information, and making sure my photo was cute but not sexy. That's where I met him, Musiq. Musiq was about 5'5, 175 pounds, attractive in his own way. He was an ex-felon (over twenty years ago) but had successfully worked for a company that facilitated event planning for major events for over ten years. His job was setting up, building stages, lighting…the works.

The first plus is that he made me laugh, no, not a cute, cover-your-mouth laugh but a fall-to-the-floor "boy you stupid" laugh. He was also a gentleman and we connected in a way that I had never had with anyone before. The only problem was that he lived in San Antonio with a female roommate.

Are you thinking the same thing I'm thinking?

After sensing my reservations, Musiq took me to San Antonio to meet this "female" roommate. Carla was a heavy-set woman who was not super friendly, probably because she had to raise her two grandkids (ages two and four) because her daughter was on drugs. When I would come and spend the night with Musiq, Carla was hardly there; she would be in and out. On the rare occasion I saw her, she would greet me and go to her room. Musiq told me Carla was his best friend from high school. He said he had dated a few of her cousins and a couple of best friends. It never worked out and they ended up blaming her because she did not tell them what he was doing. So, she was reluctant to get attached to anyone he was involved with.

Musiq spent a lot of time in Houston or out of town on gigs. We decided that it did not make sense for him to get his own place in San Antonio in order to save the money to start our own business.

During our two-year relationship, we set up a gig for Brian McKnight's concert. During one performance, Brian asked the band to stop the music because "Something's wrong with the stage." My eyes got big and locked with Musiq's eyes. Brian began to walk in my direction – I was frozen, asking myself why he was walking towards me and not Musiq. I handled all the clerical duties while Musiq was hands on. What did he think I could do? I looked in the direction I last saw Musiq, and he was no longer there. Suddenly a bright light was turned on me and, when I turned back around, there he was, Musiq, on one knee as Brian McKnight began to his song, *Everything*. There in front of everyone, he asked to marry me. I gladly accepted!

We ended up buying our own equipment and started our own business, Party Remix, where we would set up for big parties and events. We created a website, a Facebook and Instagram page and had over 5000 followers. We were known on all social media sites as the "Go-getter" couple. This was extremely important to me because of the line of work I was in. It helped me use my relationship to inspire not only the juvenile girls that I worked with but also my own children. I even had women in my inbox asking me for advice on relationships. We were an open book: we posted everything we did on social media, never to brag but to encourage and inspire. I was very happy being a part of something Black people could look up to. I still believe that a big part of our success was being a Black couple, being transparent about how we loved one another, made money together and had fun doing it. I encouraged Musiq for us to go commercial to help brand our business, and it WORKED! We made all sorts of goofy commercials, doing skits and even danced. We definitely became a household name. We even inspired his best friend Chris and his wife to start a food truck, though, unfortunately, his wife's enthusiasm burned out when she caught Chris cheating – I don't blame her one bit!

Life was good. My career was flourishing, our business was growing we had begun traveling all across Texas setting up big events for major artists and a host of other talents.

That was until I received a call late one night. I peeked at the clock with one eye. It was11:11p.m. I felt around in the dark for my cell phone. You don't want no problems, no problems with me at that hour.

Me: Hello (in a raspy voice).

Caller: Sniff, sniff.

Me: Hello (with a whole attitude).

Caller: Sniff, sniff.

I take the phone away from my ear to look at the contact name – Bae Sis? WHAT is Carla doing calling this late?

Me: Carla???!!!

Carla: Yea, sorry for waking you up, but I just couldn't take it anymore. I'm tired of the lies, I'm tired of him!!! I told him. I told him. I told him if he came back over here again disrespecting me…using me. I'm so tired of him using me!! If he's supposed to be marrying you, then we can't do this anymore. I told him I was gonna call you and tell you everything!!! I can't believe he put his hands on me!! That's why I called the cops!!

Me: Girl, What?? Who are you talking about?? Musiq??!!

Carla: YES!! You'd better come get him – the cops are on the way!

Me: WHATTTT???! (I stand up so fast, I knock over my wine glass from earlier). What are you saying???

Carla: Musiq will NEVER marry you. (She hangs up.)

What the Jerry Springer mess is this??

NOT AGAIN!!!

To be Continued…

About the Author

D. Washington is a 12-year Veteran of the U.S. Air Force and has dedicated 30 years to the medical field. She also currently works in the entertainment industry and supports issues facing Black women. Her most valuable accomplishments to date are being the mother of her two beautiful children and being "Hunni Dee" to her 3.5 grandchildren.

To contact the author, please send an email to ddarque@hotmail.com.